Vote for Me

ALL ABOUT CIVICS

Written by Kirsten Hall

Illustrated by Bev Luedecke

children's press®

A Division of Scholastic Inc.
New York Toronto London Auckland Sydney
Mexico City New Delhi Hong Kong
Danbury, Connecticut

About the Author

Kirsten Hall, formerly an early-childhood teacher,
is a children's book editor in New York City. She has been
writing books for children since she was thirteen years old
and now has over sixty titles in print.

About the Illustrator

Bev Luedecke enjoys life and nature in Colorado.
Her sparkling personality and artistic flair are reflected in her
creation of Beastieville, a world filled with lovable Beasties
that are sure to delight children of all ages.

Library of Congress Cataloging-in-Publication Data

Hall, Kirsten.
  Vote for me : all about civics / written by Kirsten Hall ;
illustrated by Bev Luedecke.
      p. cm.
Summary: As class elections approach, all the Beasties consider their
special qualities.
   ISBN 0-516-22897-8 (lib. bdg.)   0-516-24658-5 (pbk.)
   [1. Elections–Fiction. 2. Schools–Fiction. 3. Stories in rhyme.] I.
Luedecke, Bev, ill. II. Title.
   PZ8.3.H146Vo 2003
   [E]–dc21
                              2003001580

A NOTE TO PARENTS AND TEACHERS

Welcome to the world of the Beasties, where learning is FUN. In each of the charming stories in this series, the Beasties deal with character traits that every child can identify with. Each story reinforces appropriate concept skills for kindergartners and first graders, while simultaneously encouraging problem-solving skills. Following are just a few of the ways that you can help children get the most from this delightful series.

Stories to be read and enjoyed

Encourage children to read the stories aloud. The rhyming verses make them fun to read. Then ask them to think about alternate solutions to some of the problems that the Beasties have faced or to imagine alternative endings. Invite children to think about what they would have done if they were in the story and to recall similar things that have happened to them.

Activities reinforce the learning experience

The activities at the end of the books offer a way for children to put their new skills to work. They complement the story and are designed to help children develop specific skills and build confidence. Use these activities to reinforce skills. But don't stop there. Encourage children to find ways to build on these skills during the course of the day.

Learning opportunities are everywhere

Use this book as a starting point for talking about how we use reading skills or math or social studies concepts in everyday life. When we search for a phone number in the telephone book and scan names in alphabetical order or check a list, we are using reading skills. When we keep score at a baseball game or divide a class into even-numbered teams, we are using math.

The more you can help children see that the skills they are learning in school really do have a place in everyday life, the more they will think of learning as something that is part of their lives, not as a chore to be borne. Plus you will be sending the important message that learning is fun.

Madeline Boskey Olsen, Ph.D.
Developmental Psychologist

Bee-Bop

Puddles

Slider

Wilbur

Pip & Zip

Flippet

Pooky

Mr. Rigby

We're the Beasties

Smudge

Toggles

Mr. Rigby has big news.
"Everyone, please come in here!

It is time to have a vote!"
All the students start to cheer.

"You must choose a president.
I hope that each of you will run.

Everyone can vote just once.
This job can be a lot of fun!"

Bee-Bop calls out, "Vote for me!
I can read! I am so smart!"

Toggles hopes to win the vote.
"I will fill this room with art!"

Puddles knows what she will do.
"Vote for me and I will spray!"

Zip and Pip hope they will win.
"We will work hard every day!"

Wilbur does not want to run.
"Oh, but Wilbur, you must try!"

Flippet has a nice, big sign.
"Vote for me and we can fly!"

Pooky has some yummy plans.
"Who wants berry pies for lunch?

I can make all sorts of things!
I can make you berry punch!"

Smudge does not know what to do.
He does not know what to say.

He does not have any plans.
He thinks very hard all day.

"What can I do that is great?
I cannot think of anything!"

"You can hug and you can smile."
"You can push friends on the swing!"

"You can reach things way up high!"
"You make sure to always share!"

"You are always there to help!"
"You are always very fair!"

Smudge looks at his friends and smiles.
"I guess that I will run then, too!"

"We hope you feel better now.
Everything we said was true!"

All the votes have been turned in.
Mr. Rigby counts each one.

"Smudge, it is good that you ran.
It is clear that you have won!"

Smudge looks up. "I really won?"
He falls right off his great big chair!

"I cannot believe I won!"
"We all want you because you care!"

COUNTING GAME

Pooky thinks her berry pies will
help her win the big vote!

1. How many berry pies can you count?

2. How many cups of berry punch do you see?

3. How many students are eating?

4. How many students are drinking?

SOUNDS LIKE...

"Fine" sounds like "sign".
What other words do you know
that sounds like "sign"?

LET'S TALK ABOUT IT

Everyone wants to win the election.

1. Why do you think Smudge won?

2. Do you think the class made a good decision?

3. What would you say about yourself if you were trying to win?

4. How would you feel if you won a class election? What if you didn't?

WORD LIST

a	clear	help	off	sign	true
all	come	here	oh	smart	try
always	counts	high	on	smile	turned
am	day	his	once	smiles	up
and	do	hope	one	Smudge	very
any	does	hopes	out	so	vote
anything	each	hug	pies	some	votes
are	every	I	Pip	sorts	want
art	everyone	in	plans	spray	wants
at	everything	is	please	start	was
be	fair	it	Pooky	students	way
because	falls	job	president	sure	we
Bee-Bop	feel	just	Puddles	swing	what
been	fill	know	punch	that	who
believe	Flippet	knows	push	the	Wilbur
berry	fly	looks	Rigby	then	will
better	for	lot	ran	there	win
big	friends	lunch	reach	they	with
but	fun	make	read	things	won
calls	good	me	really	think	work
can	great	Mr.	room	thinks	you
cannot	guess	must	run	this	yummy
care	hard	news	said	time	Zip
chair	has	not	say	to	
cheer	have	now	share	Toggles	
choose	he	of	she	too